# THE BRIGADE'S LOVE STORM

## THE MILITANT LOVE WAR

SUMEET KUMAR

*Sumeet Kumar*

**Sumeet Kumar** , A adult who experiences many phases of love in his life , get broked many times , stands up every time and keep moving to the next phases of the life.In reality he is a writter as well as singer (as a hobby).

Very exciting and interesting fact about him is that he is aauthor of New era i.e. he starts his journey of writing at the age when he was going to schools to get the study . His some famous works i.e. Maturity Of Love (Genre - Love),Privacy For Dream (Genre - Middle Class), Army Squad ofLove (Genre- The Seperation of Army Love), 5 Days of Love(Genre- Temporarily Love), Th e Endearment Of Love(Genre - Historical Era Of Love), Social Destruction Indo-Pak (Genre - The Story of The Love At The Time Of Division Of India And Pakistan), Middle Class Soul (Genre - The Dreams of Middle Class), The Accursed Kanatpur (Genre -The Horrific Story Of A Village), Wrong Number (Genre -The Suspenseful Physco Killer Story), The Secrecy OfDeadly Midnight (Genre - The Suspense About a Crime),Fragile Religious Of Death (Genre- The Death Of A TrustfulPerson), Nature Vs Science (Genre - The Future Battle Between Nature And Science In A Horrific Way), Generic Man (Genre - The Dream of I.I.T), The Unconsious 12 Hours(Genre - The Illusion At Stage Of Comma), The StrangeBurden (Genre - The Burden Of Love) , Her Existence (Genre- The Female Pain In The Society) , Jockstrap Prize (Genre -The True Story Of A National Athlete) , H Man [Hindi] (Genre - Superhero Tragic Story), H Man [English] (Genre - Superhero Tragic Story) , Maturity Of Love [Englsih] (Genre - Love) and many more are available on various geners on the offcial platform of **Amazon, Flipkart and Notionpress**. You can buy them from there.

# Contents

# PREFACE

It is said that there are many situations in life, it all seems easy when someone is there to support, there is no reason for love because it is just an exorcism, the feet to erase someone's silence, when the same thing applies to the feet, then this is the way Whose fate also passes through each other's death, no one in the whole world feels it from his family, even if he is his own nafs, never take a break from him, because that is his whole life in the right way. Now-a-days, if it were so easy in any road, then Laila, Majnu, Ranjha would never wish to give herself a path for the sake of her love. Even when their soul were with each other, they never realized that they are the reason for living for each other, whose desire is the death of any common man, when we love this for some reason, then we have to this happy time. Even imagination didn't say that his words are for us to say. For the people, the country will become the reason for the right enmity. With time, each one becomes small, such toh that no one is suppressed, nor has any narration of it been done by anyone. Even the witness is more than them, the tradition of his fanna also starts when there is a word of plan , even only the property of which we were never the owner because this property is God's name, it is in the name of the above person who has entrusted it to us. Everyone asks for this right from you because he wants it because if the desire was there, then desires would have disappeared. This is not true, because in the world everyone says peace, they say that where there is a shadow of humanity, that cruelty is definitely there somewhere or the other. If someone proves wrong, such truth has not remained till today, we are in the world. Why should we do the conversation of other country when the humanity of your country is not in our rights because nowadays every person's pond is related to some politics, everyone is only and only Farrowg's desire , not of humanity at all, it has become the word of camels. We have determined our own limits and we are putting a rock in the face of others.

# ACKNOWLEDGEMENTS

*Aman Kumar*

Special Thanks to **Aman Kumar** who worked so hard in the preparation of this book. He has continually put with my passive voice, omission of words, and late night calls. You have be en wonderful. Thanks to him for his precious time in reviewing proposals , individual chapters and early drafts, along with his suggestions on the applicability of the material to the world.

# I
# The Firing Of War

Here everyone is definitely aware of the name of humanity, but when it comes to fulfilling humanity, then everyone takes their steps backward, saying that it should be our government, why should it be its people , maybe it should not be there because it is not in it. I am different from no one nor have it been told that there is one thing in the feet of separation, so that humanity is against it, someone says that it is cash against it; No one gets harmed in Jung. I have already mentioned that feet, what kind of damage is done to shapes of humanity , just look at it, any sister hides her tears in the day when she returns to her clothes. Comes a mother calls her in the shadow of Apnemanta when she comes to her country by giving her life A brother wakes up gracefully and the very next day he enlists in the army to save his mother India.made the name of our world whose name is called India today. The reason for his death is only one, that too only and only to save his country and in return he never wanted anything from us, this is the politics of our country. Keeping feet to me, it is never a matter of society, till today, what have we done for them, in what condition is the family, have we ever felt the need to ask them because with the passage of time, we forget their sacrifice as well, because of Bhagat Singh. Marty should be remembered, we believe in Valentine's Day, I have not wronged everyone, do whatever it is right to do, because where war has a tradition, it should be done without love, I am of the same rot in my feet and I want to do this thing. I am wrong because the one who gave his whole youth in the name of his country so that he killed his love affair and also surrendered his love to the mother who gave birth to him in front of his country. I can only say that Bash can say that even if you do love Chim because it's the way it is told Even then, it happened only because of the soldiers of our country, because if they had not lived, we would not have had this country, and if we did not have this country, then how would you narrate love and think that my words have also faded in front of the love story, who left his unrelenting love behind. I chose to defend my country.

*""Neither do I wish for any love, nor do I keep a*
*pond for it,*
*I love the tricolor of my country, for whose*
*protection I can die every day....*
*We have a desire to save the country and no*
*matter how hard our work is,*
*we have the power to eradicate it every*
*time............."*"

# II
# The Soul Deatches

It is said that there is no limit in war because even if it is one sided, it will never allow its tradition to happen and even if it is two sided, its tradition will not stop in front of anyone, all the pains in the pond of time. Everyone goes somewhere and gets cured. There is some pain in the feet, whose worship is also pain in the world and its ending is also pain. If you spend your whole life thinking about yourself, then it is not called life because even though his birth is separate, when he comes to the world, then his existence does not remain separate. In reality, only those relationships are true, who support you while casting your shadow with you, and in reality, humanity is said to protect each other and end with their grace, well if we play the same thing like a game of words. If they stay, their love story will remain, because of which they do war for the countries in the world of love, she completely ended because of her love. Toh shish story started from the city of Gwalior in Punjab (1970) Neither there is mention of any Heer and Ranjhe in the mirror story nor any laila mjanu in the mirror story. It is because this story is of those two love souls, who sacrificed their love for the country without any thought, so their story started at the time when both of them were very innocent, the hero of the special story is our Jagveer and the heroine of our story The love story of Jagveer and Gunakeerat started when they did not even know each other properly, I mean, they have never been able to meet each other's existence, this love story is a little different hyper such a love story, neither has anyone ever heard nor Anyone must have ever seen because even though both the bodies were the same foot they were still not aware of each other's existence. So the story really started when he was born that too on the same day and in the same speech also. Wahe guru himself had written his fate, the feet say that if a destination is very close to you and you have to be happy at the right time. Not even her oblivion, not even her pond, even her pond changes her luck for a while, she will never be separated from your existence because she says that even if she doesn't come, she stays the same even if each other's words are not right.

It was because they were not only capable of meeting each other's truth and at the same time, Gunkeerat's father was also in the army and Jagveer's father was also in the army. They never met each other as I already said this is not a common story then (1970) ) At the time, I do not know any boundary at that time because I myself was innocent, so enough can hardly say that there was a pond in the evening and there was a different day in the panel. Another accident happened at the time of his birth that both of them were in a hospital. Even when I was there, I did not meet them. Jagveer and Gunkeerat's father were not present at the time of their birth because at that time the image of war was such that they were forced. Because no matter how much trouble comes to his family, still he knows about his country. They think that they keep the pond of protection of their mother land in the forefront, such a thing is reconnaissance that they all do not have families, they do not have any festivals, they leave all of them, and only you wake up day and night for mother India and protect them. This is where a common man is concerned about his life and he always thinks about himself, about his family first, the soldiers of our country think about the country first because they always say that they are the best. Be that no matter how many troubles their family is going through, their preference is always that our brothers and sisters should never face any trouble and their homes should always be safe, even if their houses are burnt, even if they do not burn. Why don't the family stay in the silence of the darkness, they first think about us that the lamps of our house are not there, the silence in the walls of their house is not that thing in the house of our brothers and sisters, neither they always There is only one person who believes that even if we are given the blessings of our house, I will not allow this tradition to happen in the homes of any brother in the country. Time passes, but many times pass, yet their preference will never change for our country and will never change. Intelligence is also enough work to give an example of their valor. He never recommended anything to his country, nor did he ever call him wrong in the condition where a common man narrates the tirade of his fellow man, and our soldiers tell us to always keep us safe, wouldn't they have dreams that they too They don't have their dreams, don't they have love, they don't have the love of mother's love, in spite of all this, why do they all live with leisure, after all, they have thought about the most important thing, where we strengthen our home shapes . Brother, he protects the country with his blood, he never cares about his life because he surrenders his soul to his country from the very day on which he says the promise of saving the sheep and also of the mirror thing. It is clear that even if we lose our lives, we are on our country's feet .No trouble will come. The word of his path always becomes his tradition because the day he steps on the border, his soul goes to our tricolour. If we look at the love story of Gunakeerat and Jagveer, then on this day both of them had the highest duty of their father's own country because their thinking was always that wherever we go we will ever go alone because the soil of the country is always sixty one of us and His father's wish was also that if we meet the path, then we should meet in our soil, say that it is of trust, it should be said that we are on the male side also we are a family and on the other side also we are a family. It could not be overcome, but the love that he had for his children was clearly visible from the handwriting of his words. Even Dr. No matter what, he never reveals the reason for happiness because he has to take care of his country, he has to protect his mother India. Then after all, in reality, the story of Gunkeerat and Jagveer begins now. They were not able to meet each other. Even after meeting, neither their families have been able to meet each other, nor Gunkeerat and Jagveer's story, which is still pending, till then, because whatever is going to happen next, whatever Wahe guru has written in their destiny. He is the spiritual master and he himself knows because I am the only way to make him aware of his immortal love story.

*"That you should do politics because we love our*
*tricolour, and if possible,*
*Be aware of your own desire, which you call*
*politics these days, because its desire is also the*
*army, Nowadays we are the slave of our tricolor...*
*...*
*that even if you will have a pond of water, feet,*
*we still love the soil of our country which has*
*given birth to us."*

# III

# The New Identity

Type of freedom but the love is look like a prisoner"
Emotions are the wall in the army, which a soldier can
never say, he can keep his wish, no further pond if he
becomes aware of this, then how will he protect his
country It is not that they do not have any kind of favor, if
there is no grace, then the country which does the gifts of

humanity today, probably negates because if we want to learn humanity from any witness, then only and only the soldiers of our country can teach anyone. No, there is only one mind for their humanity, feet are Jagveer and Gunkeerat so that love has a limit, if you are not able to meet your love in love, then divorce does not work for your restlessness, only the one who started these fictions It is that he is not angry, , he could not get to know each other, now time has come, tired of the fate that the same guru has written in his favor, now he has to do his kindly society, that with time the walls of love become stronger. They become incapable, they are also sitting in love with each other, if something else happens, then they are saved in their love story. There are no specialties of water, so there is no point in being aware of it, feet have some different hiccups in their youth, they say that if there is something written in fate, it will remain so and Waheguru has toh Jagveer and Gunkeerat's luck together. I still remember that Jagveer met Junkeerat on that day when we all went to Diljit's marriage Well, in their love story, Diljit had a big hand because Diljit's marriage would have been at the right time, perhaps Jagveer would have never been met with Gunkeerat . Can't get it because it was the last day of Gunkeerat in Gwalior, so I don't know the reason why whatever happened in the middle of each day, Diljitte Deviah, maybe I don't want to make him aware of pronunciation desire, so I will take you all directly on his way. On this day, it happened that Jagveer was not at all that he went to Diljit's marriage, took him forcibly in her marriage, but the first time Jagveer met him with gusto gunkeert, whose fate had been written long ago by Waheguru. Feet coincidentally the words and then Never made them aware, both of them also do not know why they used to not know each other because at the time they were very close to each other, yet Najagveer saw him and neither did Gunkeerat even before his feet had said that luck gave handwriting that too That can never fade away Well, let me make you aware of some mishaps in connection with the rituals of meeting, so Hades , Diljit's father and our maternal uncle rakhi this in front of the girl's people, saying that their Veera, I mean Diljeete, to go Abroad, along with ten lakh rupees DFA. In the Suzuki car too, the people of the feet girls refused it and said that bricks ,money ,we cant give foot five lakh cash and Suzuki car is ready to give, meanwhile our uncle said that it is if such thing then my son couldnt marriage with your daughter , then will the girl's family members also be sad and their brides maids will also win our hearts and why not because both the love was true, let Mamaji understand enough uncle , he gave his son lsitened and were asked to know back and on the other hand, the girl's father threatened that if my daughter is not married, then your son will not be able to go two feet, Dharam raj, our mother's name was Dharam raj, so that he did not kill anyone. Didn't do religion and he was conceited, he was living with his son and also with your daughter in law when the girl's father said that if your son will not marry my daughter, so today your son will not able to save . (I don't mind hearing this, how can he see tears in her eyes with the love with which he has brought up his daughter and this was probably also necessary because it was his daughter's talk and for his blood, someone would have his birth) Can even give to take the life of someone , that too for the one with whom he is very infatuated, that too when his daughter's happiness has come to his feet, how will he let her go like this, so taking someone's life is a matter of time, isn't it? Then what was the temperature of our mother increased and she also gave it that Merveera will also be saved and her Bapu will also die. we are also married and hear you bajaj ,do whatever you want to do no need to tell about anyone , yet this is the girl's father. The fight had escalated to such an extent that both of them had torn each other's feet with guns and even those who were married All of them were present, they had cut out and what can I say about all the women who were like us, they do not have the desire to kill anyone because their language is enough for anyone, that day the atmosphere of work and jung is very different. It was because all the men were holding guns at each other and all the women were abusing each other, and we could have done anything by talking about us, except to see, the thing is that the man is Jagveer. I was nowhere to be seen, even though he had come with me when the legs started fighting, he had disappeared somewhere, I had seen gunkeerat, our hero was missing in the midst of so many places, this thing was disturbing me because we are our own We can't even move from the place, because the girl's people had pointed guns at us and we are not a jamisbend who be in action mode all the time and dare to save yourself that too when our life is hard at gun point, then in all we have forgotten one thing that only one hero survives in every story, so how can that tradition disappear in love story When this battle was running uncountably, then our hero entered from the main gate (and everyone knows that when a hero dies, the entire script of the film changes, that too something similar happened). Mane Parjagvir's talk, he never used to avoid because Jagvirunka was a lovely nephew among all of us and yes because he was such a boy who had chosen to live as Hefrogh since childhood, he was completely different from his brother, for Jagveer's Bapu country. used to protect him, our hero was our life, he always thought about his family, the only boy in the house who had taken over the business of his house from the age of ten because he used to be so infatuated with Jagveer's father's duty that he never lost his business. Didn't pay attention. Let's see what happens after the entry of our hero. When Jagveer came, he himself was surprised that he was just walking happily sometime back and so quickly turned into a war undefined when everyone told him that because of uncle demand, he was in our condition. Changed, son ,uncle , even if I told anyone, I never used to avoid the talk of Jagveer, and he had no reason to refuse becaus our brother , our Jagveer was everyone's life, it was Qian, it was the reason for this. Even before you will know soon, listen to what he said and see. On this day, our brother said the same thing to the mother that human beings are worried about humanity. It is because of him that the handwriting of the poor people coming, the handwriting of the pages may be lost even at the time, the happiness that you do today, you never change the sweet times, the feet should not be a human being, there should not be any problem of the amount, mother, it seems like a prisoner in life. It is and this girl's price is only for Bapu to know. Your hero will not be able to be happy tomorrow, and you will not be able to express your love to your soulmate. When Jagveer said these words, everyone went to the society after listening to it, and because of this, the life got entangled. Directly on the heart of Waqtgunkeerat, because of which Gunkeerat has, at the time of his heart's love, could not meet our brother of name card and tehn time will also far from them , because only after that he was gone in a while, because of this why he had gone. We were all human feet, because of the things he had said, we finally got it done and asked for our uncle and Bajaj uncle along with us. Veere has put it, I mean the beginning of Jishkashish, our Veere has started for his virtue, what is his strength? Will they make a new destination? Will they be able to create a new destination, even if they don't love each other? You will know soon, till then you will know about your life.

> *"It is a coincidence that I am aware of all the*
> *writings of love,*
> *and I know that I want: even today,*
> *I am happy with your bad habit.*
> *Entire life has passed. There is a huge pond.*
> *Knowing its love gives me the reason for the*
> *path and neither the prayer to stay alive."*

# IV

# The Disunion

So Capture the Humanity for my country" Love doesn't
have meaning in the existence of love, only had heard it
somewhere before when our Veere met with virtuousness,
so in those days, the eyes also saw his efforts, its tradition
started when the poet won hearts.it had happened the very
next day, I mean the wedding day the next day the
destination of Gunkeerat was somewhere else, because of

the conversation of the feet of the world, there is only one heather, which we call love, even though each other is also capable of happy times. Even when it had not happened, Gunkeerat's eyes were looking like a rage of love for Jagveer. It was only because of this that the word had changed to the extent that Gunkeerat had never in his entire life, now he was going to happen, something happened. Shakti was Veer's sister's very good friend. promise seems to be full (elder brother) For a moment, it is Gunkeerat first. What has happened, what to do, love is such a thing, it is not aware of anyone's thinking, nor what was the relationship between them, so his lust didn't work at the time, so his love for Jagveer was straight from him. Can you get me to meet your vada filled then? Have you said why didn't you even bother to ask why you didn't get my vada filled then? One reason behind it is that first they worshiped, they were both friends. It was also a matter of fact that both were firm friendships, but sometimes their relationship is bigger than their own, when the beginning has already begun, it is necessary to mix luck, not when the bride has gone, everyone has come back to their homes. Even when he came to his house, he was not our deserted, it was also the matter of Raan that Gunakirt was permanent for us, also only and only to meet nrother then , no one had any news that Jagveer is where he was asking all the time Jagveer Even in marriage, Jagveer did not show up even in the night, lately Jagveer also went there, mother now asked that where was the son till late, Jagveer was yesterday Even in the wedding night, I saw the same answer as our Veere's answer was that that mother was a necessary task, so I had to go to Para. And brother said that it will complete , mother said this son is all yours please, you don't explain to us tomorrow, oh yours brother of Life gets spoiled, our brother said that you don't even need to think about all this, no matter what, I have talked about him going Abroad, Sharmaji will make all those arrangements. Then what was the time to mother? It was feeling that you are our last hope, our hero is getting applause. Aysha was that no one can do jealousy, one could go against her, one mistake in all this was that Gunakeerat had also seen that she stopped herself and directly hugged our heroine that such a problem should stand Gone were the times, which no one expected, brother was surprised, all the logs she was there were surprised that who is this after all? Never seen what was it, everyone started making that beats, she didn't even pinch to tell that this is my childhood friend. Then everyone started asking her why are you hugging our Veere girl? Seh did not think earlier that he is not only Jagveer but our entire family is also present, there were many good times at the time, why did not you all say that when the surgery women of the locality together ask you this question. Who is obviously the right thing, you will not be afraid, nor do I know everything about everyone. Most of all said that you don't worry, this is my childhood friend, she is a resident of city next to us, there was some work so she has come to meet me and there is no cheek and why should you stay in your body, go bride has come home to welcome her undefined then What was it after that no one even looked back at Gunkeerat. Because everyone knew that our heroic can't do any wrong. And even if he did a mistake, even then he did not support anyone, someone told him something. What was said by everyone's great gunkeerat went up to the limit for brother , which had no limit. Heather has got a pinch, what are you doing, I want to welcome the new bride of the bridegroom with me. In the same way, I should also become like my brother . On this day, they may not be able to meet each other well. Will see it and it has some work, let's go, sit and sit, I will roam around in my city. Now in reality, their love story was going to happen where the helplessness of Gunkirt was so much that she was in our house where she did not talk about her heart in front of brother . small and Gunakeerat made this plan that on the first morning when our brother gets out of work, then Gunakeerat will also go with her and that's it is closing. Foot question is still many whether Gunkeerat told his heart to Jagveer, and after being called in the army, did they ever meet and when did Jagveer meet Gunkeerat then and if he used to love her as much So why did he never talk to her about it and when they both belonged to the same body, why didn't they digest each other and neither did his family and the last question was who am I related to Jagveer? that the handwriting of many pages is still undefined, which of them seems to be right next, let's see the foot in the next part of it.

*"Even if I am going to leave your destination,*
*if possible, then if we return it in time, then it is*
*okay and if it does not return by chance,*
*then take care of my dear mother, who is still*
*waiting for the return of her son.*
*Seeing the grace of my military brothers, they*
*stand proudly in the sun, protecting the country.*
*This is not just a wish for the competition for*
*our enemies."*